ALAN ACKERMAN IS STILL MISSING

A SHORT MYSTERY STORY

ALEXANDRIA BLAELOCK

Also by Alexandria Blaelock

SHORT STORY COLLECTIONS
The Histories of Hayward Hall
Lovelorn, Lovestruck and Love at First Sight
Common or Garden Variety Heroes
Case Files of the Wilkinson Detective Agency
Unavoidable Fates
Christmas Travesties
Five Faces of Felicia Clarke
Little Place Called Home
Security Directorate Dossiers v. 1.

FICTION
That Love Nonsense
Taipan vs Brown
The Ghost and Ms Cox
Friends Like That

MS BLAELOCK'S BOOKS
Stress Free Dinner Parties
Signature Wardrobe Planning
Holistic Personal Finance
Minimally Viable Housekeeping
Planning a Life Worth Living

PICTURE BOOKS
Australia Felix

A SELECTION OF AVAILABLE SHORT STORIES
Alma's Grace
Morning Star, Evening Star, Superstar
Shining Star
Ship in a Bottle
Simone Says Hands in the Air

ALAN ACKERMAN IS STILL MISSING

A SHORT MYSTERY STORY

ALEXANDRIA BLAELOCK

BlueMere Books
MELBOURNE, AUSTRALIA

Publisher's Note: This is a work of fiction. Names, characters, places, and incidents are a product of the author's imagination. Locations and public names are sometimes used for atmospheric purposes. Any resemblance to actual people, living or dead, or to businesses, companies, events, institutions, or locations is completely coincidental.

For permission requests, please contact enquiries@bluemerebooks.com.

Ordering Information:
Discounts are available on quantity purchases. For details, contact orders@bluemerebooks.com.

Alan Ackerman is Still Missing/Alexandria Blaelock
paperback ISBN: 978-1-922744-69-2
digital ISBN: 978-1-923083-00-4

Book Layout © BookDesignTemplates.com
Cover Art: topographical map © yamonstro/Depositphotos, and man silhoette © Michal Sanca/Depositphotos

ALAN ACKERMAN
IS STILL MISSING

It was the day before Alan Ackerman flew across the country to start University.

Summer was dying, and we'd taken the train to the Fremantle beach so we could be alone for one last time before he left. Somewhere far away from his disapproving parents.

They'd let him spend time with me while we were still at school, though they didn't know about the necking behind the bike sheds.

Or maybe they did.

Their opinion would've been he needed to get all his wild oat sowing done before he met a "nice" girl from a "good" family and settled into a life befitting his station.

As it turned out, they correctly assumed he'd tire of slumming it with me, Hazel Riggs, and move on.

That last day was hot, but not too hot. We'd arrived late in the afternoon, just in time to watch the Mums pack up their kids to go home and cook lovely dinners for their Dads.

It wasn't long before the beach was an endless strip of sand inhabited only by seagulls, empty chip packets and discarded soft drink cans.

We swam, we kissed, and after drinking some of the beer Alan brought in his backpack, he took my virginity.

Seems banal now, but at the time, it was truly magical.

The setting sun coloured the sky in shades of pink and purple.

We lay in a pool of cool dune cast shade. The sound of the surf roared in our ears, and the taste of salt on our bodies as the light, seaweed tainted breeze raised goosebumps on our lightly burnt skin.

We ate the tomato sandwiches I'd made with white bread because I didn't know any better, but pink by the time we ate them.

He was more emotional than me, perhaps because he was the one leaving on a new adventure while I was staying home to get a job and take care of my ageing parents.

There's something so pitiful about those of us who willingly sacrificed our futures for those who've already lived their lives to the full. Poor darlings, we didn't know any better.

Alan was torn between the comfortable and conventional life he was leaving behind, and the frisson of danger in moving out on his own so far away.

He needed a life raft to cling to, and for the time being, that life raft was me.

"We should meet up in fifteen years," he said.

I don't know why he said fifteen, not ten or twenty.

Uni plus ten, I suppose.

"We've been watching too many old movies," I replied, "you'll be suggesting the Empire State Building next."

He blew a raspberry. "Everyone goes there. We should meet at that castle in the cave you like so much."

"Predjama? The Yugoslavian one?"

"Yeah, that's it."

"I could do that," I said, twirling a lock of hair around my index finger.

"That's settled then," he said with a nod of his head.

"In fifteen years, we'll be thirty-two. Should we round it down to thirty?"

"Okay, that sounds better. February twenty-four, nineteen ninety-seven. The anniversary of the first time we did it!"

And then we did it again.

We were so young and foolish.

I thought a trip to New York City couldn't compare to a coach trip across the romantic European countryside to a castle that's literally part of a mountain.

Then again, I was assuming we'd be together on the coach. Seated side by side, mucking about under a blanket as we drove through a darkened landscape.

What could possibly compare to that?

Aside, perhaps, from making a date for thirteen years in the future.

And not transferring it from paper diary to paper diary, to electronic diary, to hand-held communication device, to smart phone, to online calendar, and finally back to paper again as the years went by.

Social media didn't exist in those days, so I got a job at the Country Club, where I shamelessly eavesdropped on the patron's conversations. Hoping for news about what he was up to.

Just as well. Within a year, he'd stopped replying to my letters and calling me when he came home for vacations.

He was making a success of himself, and I was cleaning up after people like him.

After a few years, I could follow his progress in the newspapers. He was busy being a success, dating starlets and eventually marrying one.

Whereas I was busy going nowhere, dating a succession of no-hopers and achieving nothing.

Even I understood by then, there was no reason someone like him would bother with someone like me.

But even though I hadn't heard from Alan in a decade, as 1996 came to a close, I quit my Country Club job, and blew the tiny inheritance my parents left me on a once in a lifetime trip to Europe.

On February 24, 1997, I was at Predjama, only by that time Predjama was in Slovenia.

It's funny isn't it, how borders and histories change over time? How they're never the fixed foundations we believe they are.

On that day, I realised the Empire State Building was, in fact, a much better choice of rendezvous. What with its one restricted entrance and small surface area.

The castle, grounds, and caves of the Postojna Park were such an enormous size it was ridiculous to think we'd have been able to find each other.

Nonetheless, I'd booked a room at the hotel, because, well, you never know, do you?

It was our anniversary, after all.

But in the end, all that happened was that I restlessly paced the castle forecourt for six hours looking for him.

Even at the tail end of the Northern winter, there were too many people, and I couldn't be sure I hadn't missed him.

I was still foolish after all that time.

Disappointed, I cut my trip short and went home, back to my ordinary life.

Cursing my childish foolishness.

I was thirty years old.

I had no job, no boyfriend, no assets, and no real future.

According to the definitions of my seventeen-year-old self, I was a loser.

One pathetic, failed suicide attempt later, I decided enough was enough, and it was time to wake the fuck up and start over.

After aceing the Public Service entrance exam, I got a job in the Library Service and studied part-time at University to get a degree.

I worked my butt off, and ten years later, I was a well-paid senior public servant with staff and a budget to manage. The *Public Service Gazette* did a piece on me, calling me a success, so that was nice.

Take that Mr and Mrs Ackerman.

But I was still single, and getting the feeling that my best years were behind me.

The Public Service is littered with women like me.

Only they're a few years older and had the misfortune to be born at a time when women had to choose between husbands and careers.

Or their careers and caring for ageing parents.

Even today, our careers are still limited by the notion men are more deserving of promotions because they have families to take care of.

As if poor Miss Jones, who cares for her parents *and* her orphaned nieces isn't more deserving of a promotion because she has more people to take care of than young Mr Peters.

Mr Peters, who got the promotion, is unmarried, and whose mother takes care of him.

Mr Peters, who is, basically a fuck-wit.

Still, I can't get into the politics of it all.

I'm a Public Servant, here to implement the Government of the day's bidding, not to have policy opinions about it.

But working in the library has its benefits.

One of which is burrowing deep into the archives beneath the main building, to monitor, review, and maintain the archival material.

It wasn't strictly my job to take care of the archives, but I liked to go down there for a couple of hours of peace and quiet now and again.

And it needed to look like I was doing something, so I often collected old newspapers and magazines to scan into the collection. A mainly mindless task that leaves me plenty of time and space to think deep thoughts for a while.

Who am I kidding? They weren't deep thoughts at all.

Joshua had asked me to marry him at one minute past midnight on New Year's Day, and I had no idea what to do about it.

I was surprised because I didn't think he liked me that much.

It was probably more that he was comfortable with me and couldn't be bothered to look for someone he was passionate about.

I'd say the mere idea of the chase was enough for him to want to take a Bex and have a good lie down.

As for me, I couldn't decide whether "settling" for Joshua was the best thing to do.

I'm sure we'd have bumped along nicely enough in the daytime, but I couldn't bring myself to imagine getting intimate with him of a night in our shared bed.

Or looking at that face in the morning before I'd had coffee.

Though I'm still fairly confident, it wouldn't have been long before the sight of him carefully cleaning his glasses with his manly handkerchiefs would make me want to break them.

All of them; glasses, fingers, and hankies.

And I'm fairly sure I'd have to make him wash his own socks and underpants - I certainly didn't like him that much.

Maybe it was time to climb the last barrier and dive headlong into crazy cat lady territory by getting a cat.

But I wondered, exactly how long did I have to let the memory of one night of teenaged passion with Alan Ackerman rule my life.

Perhaps it was because I was thinking about him I noticed his name in the newspaper I was scanning.

It was about page five - still recent enough to be of interest, but losing ground to more recent stories.

The article was about his 1997 disappearance from a Slovenian hotel...

He came after me!

At least, I assume he did.

Why else would he have been in Slovenia in February 1997, but for me?

I wondered what happened to the starlet wife.

I sat on a nearby chair and folded the pages back so I could read the story.

The general gist being he was last seen leaving a bar in the town of Postojna. With conflicting reports about getting into a car, or van or something, or walking down the street.

Some issues with the CCTV recordings and police investigation, his body never found.

Alan bloody Ackerman had been somewhere near me on the appointed day.

I couldn't be sure exactly when, because he'd been travelling alone and his disappearance wasn't reported until he didn't check out of his hotel on time.

As my mother would have said, I was all at sixes and sevens.

Should I ignore this old newspaper and marry Joshua?

Or should I give Alan Ackerman one last chance before I visited the cat sanctuary?

Maybe I should have tossed a coin, but I knew I'd keep tossing until it came up Alan, so what was the point?

I needed to know what happened to my first love.

So lucky I was a Research Librarian.

I spent the next couple of weeks searching newspaper archives, looking at missing persons records, and reviewing court records.

Officially, he was still missing, hadn't been declared dead, and his parents administered his assets. I noted their address.

Not that I cared about his assets, though I wondered, sort of, about his wife.

But not a lot.

The possibility he was alive was enough for me.

And the best place to start looking for him would have to be Slovenia.

So, as January closed, I dipped into my stash of accrued long service and annual leave and booked a few weeks off to go on an Alan hunt.

As I counted down the days, getting more and more restless, I organised a researcher in Ljubljana (a friend of a friend) to start reviewing the newspapers and official records for any mention of him.

Told Joshua to find a new girlfriend.

And forget my address and phone number.

The first week I stayed in Ljubljana to meet Janez and see what he'd found. A few more details about the investigation, but basically that Alan was still missing and his body had not been recovered.

On a whim, I asked Janez to check on missing people who'd turned up but couldn't be identified.

And then I enjoyed a few overnight trips around Slovenia and out to Croatia, Italy and Austria. Because, why not? I had a bit of time to kill.

But on February 23, I checked back into Hotel Jama.

Nothing much seemed to have changed.

I enjoyed an exquisite meal of local seasonal food, and perhaps too much wine, and then the luxury of an executive suite.

I'm a successful executive now. Did I mention that already?

My savoury buffet breakfast was delicious, and I ate a huge amount because this time, I was going to thoroughly explore the park, and caves and the castle.

Starting with a walk to, and then through the caves, before heading up to the castle.

The castle was stunning, and I was only slightly regretful I hadn't made the time to check it out the last time I was there.

As I stood on the third-floor balcony, looking out over the countryside, I felt a shiver run down my spine. I turned to look behind me and saw Alan coming towards me.

He was old.

I mean, I know I'm old, but he looked really old. Like eighty or so.

Leaning on a walking stick as he limped towards me. I've no idea how he got up all those stairs.

His hair was badly cut, and his tongue was clamped between his lips as he concentrated on taking each step, and he was moving quite fast, tattered clothes flapping behind him.

I walked towards him, "Hello Alan," I said.

"Me poznaš?" he replied.

"Alan, is that you?"

"Me poznaš?" he said again.

I shrugged my shoulders and looked around for help.

A young man approached, "he's asking if you know him."

"I do know him. Does he not know himself?"

The young man translated, and Alan danced a little from foot to foot, and let fly a torrent of words.

Slovenian words.

So as it turns out, Alan Ackerman is not dead.

He just doesn't remember anything before the day he woke up in the hospital.

When his body was discovered down a small side street, they thought he was dead, and it was just good luck that sent him to a hospital and not the morgue.

At first, they'd thought he was local, a dim-witted local at that.

Probably why they'd rushed him into surgery, and after that, they'd no real option but to put him through physical therapy.

He'd fallen in love with one of his nurses, and they'd married, and when, not much later, she got an offer for a better-paid job in a bigger city they'd moved.

The nice, respectful young man was his son, and once he'd told me, I could see the resemblance.

The family didn't know why he insisted on visiting the castle on February 24 every year. Not even Alan, or Srečo, as they named him because he was lucky to be alive.

So, I explained we'd made a date to meet in 1997, but he hadn't shown up.

"Aahh," said the boy, and relayed the information to Srečo who seemed relieved to finally know the answer.

He looked at me carefully, then looked at the boy and shrugged his shoulders, so I got the idea he had no memory of me either.

And oddly enough, that was a great relief.

The boy insisted on taking me out for a meal and quizzed me inexpertly about his father's background.

Not that I could tell him much, and what I did, I made sound like an innocent high school friendship. I invented a husband and made it plain I had no interest in being more than Srečo's friend.

And even as I lied, I realised it was true.

I didn't want him back.

My life had moved on, and I wasn't a naïve seventeen-year-old anymore. I didn't want to get tangled up in the past again.

I wasn't even sure he'd survive the move back home. Or his parents' care.

But before they left me, I gave the boy my email address, and the names and address of Alan's parents.

It struck me they hadn't looked too hard for him if I'd found him so easily.

I didn't know if the Ackermans would welcome his Slovenian family, or what the legal situation was, but I hoped they'd be happy to know what became of him.

The day before I left Slovenia, I met Janez in Ljubljana, and we went through a very short list of unidentified found people.

It wasn't that hard to identify Alan now that I knew what I was looking for.

He was pleased to have contributed to what he saw as a happy ending; a reunited family.

And I guess, given the country's unhappy socialist past, he would see the reunion as a fortunate thing, but I wasn't so sure.

Though I really hoped it would be.

I also stopped at the Australian Consulate to report my findings. Hopefully, with government intervention the Ackermans couldn't brush the Slovenians aside if they wanted to.

I hope they want to see Alan and can deal with Srečo's family, but I have my doubts.

I heard some truly awful things while I was working at the Country Club.

As for me, when I got home, I got myself a cat. A big orange and white tabby whom I call sreča, because she's lucky too.

And I met a rather charming man at the cat sanctuary. We're not dating, but now and again we meet at the beach at sunset.

THE END

ABOUT THE AUTHOR

Alexandria Blaelock writes stories, some of them for *Ellery Queen's Mystery Magazine* and *Pulphouse Fiction Magazine.*

She's also written five self-help books applying business techniques to personal matters like getting dressed, cleaning house, and feeding your friends.

Discover more at https://alexandriablaelock.com.

Why not try *Taipan vs Brown*

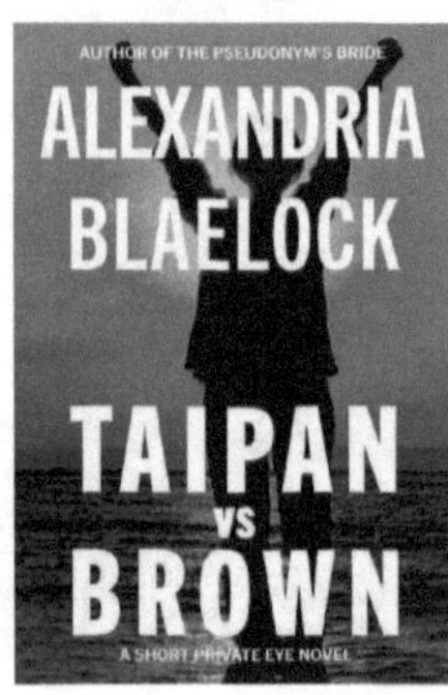

The Robin Hood of Private Detectives
Georgia Garside. Foul-mouthed Private
Investigator. Ex-contorionist.
Out of her depth. In over her head.
Caught up in the war between a wealthy
industrialist and the ex-sugar babe who can't take a
hint.
A laugh-out-loud tripartite battle of wits, winner
takes all.